The Snake

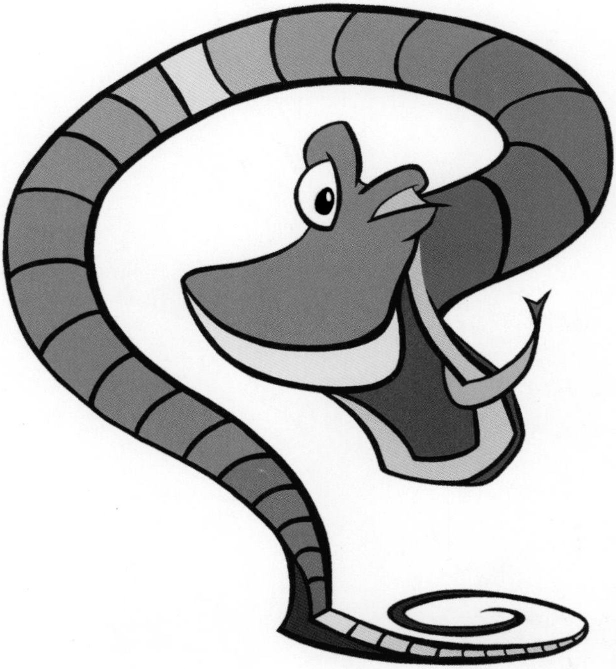

Illustrated by Josh Dobson

Rigby

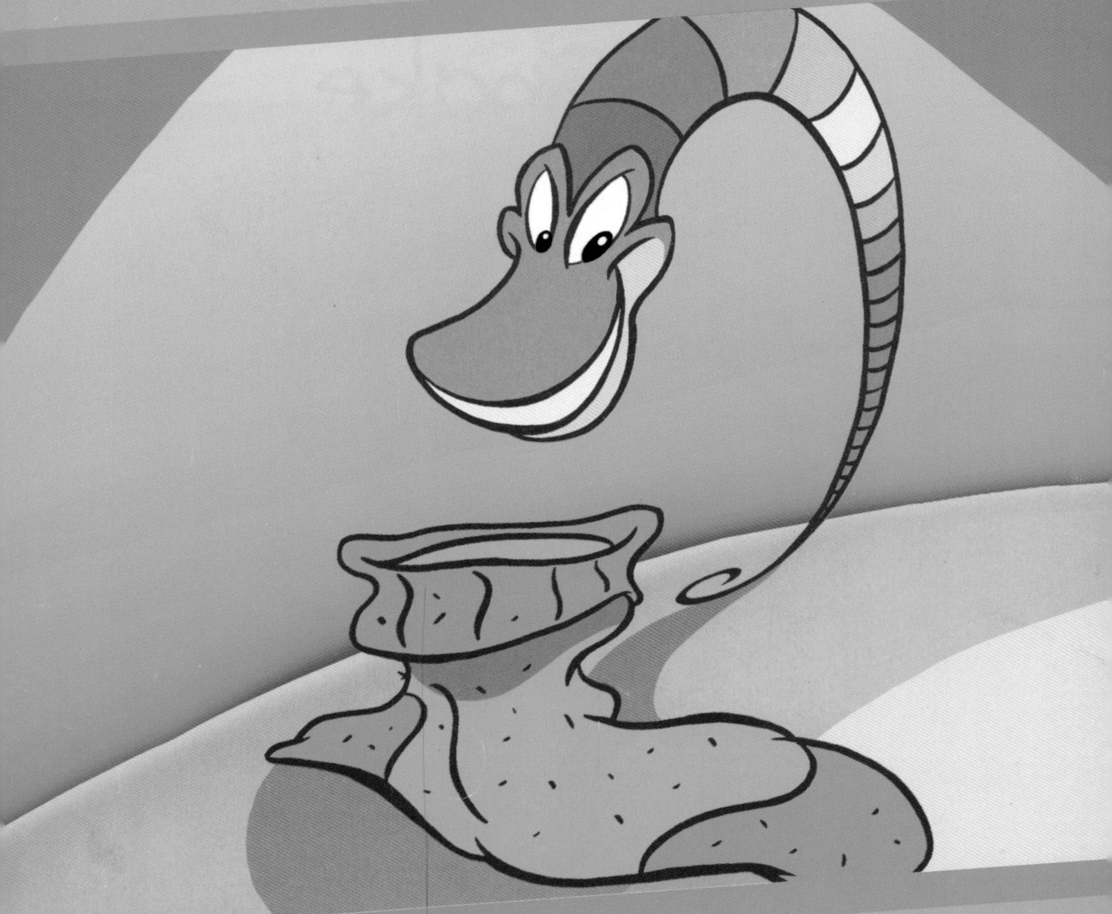

I went in the sock.

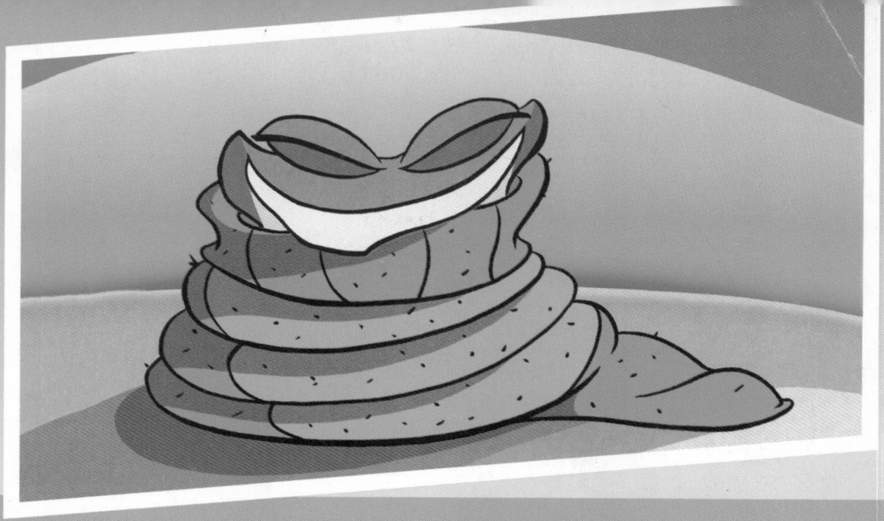

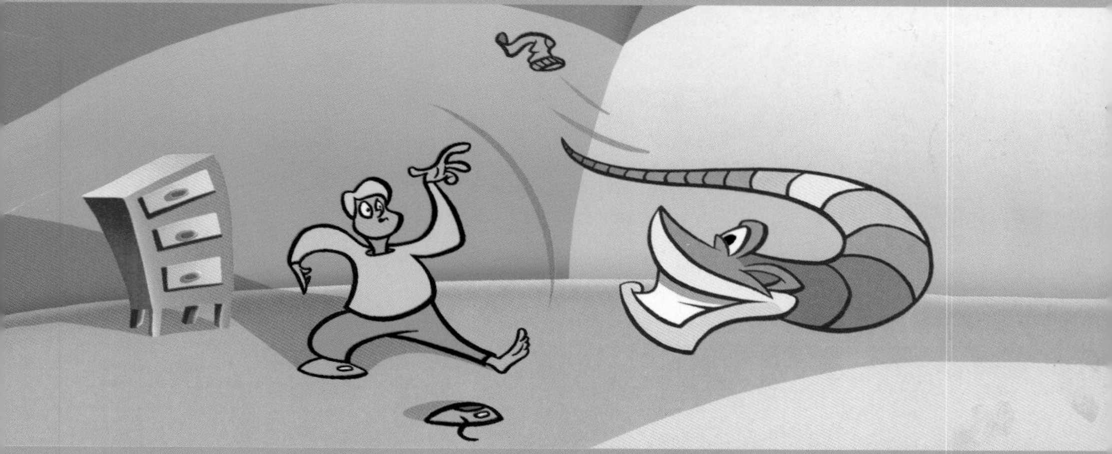

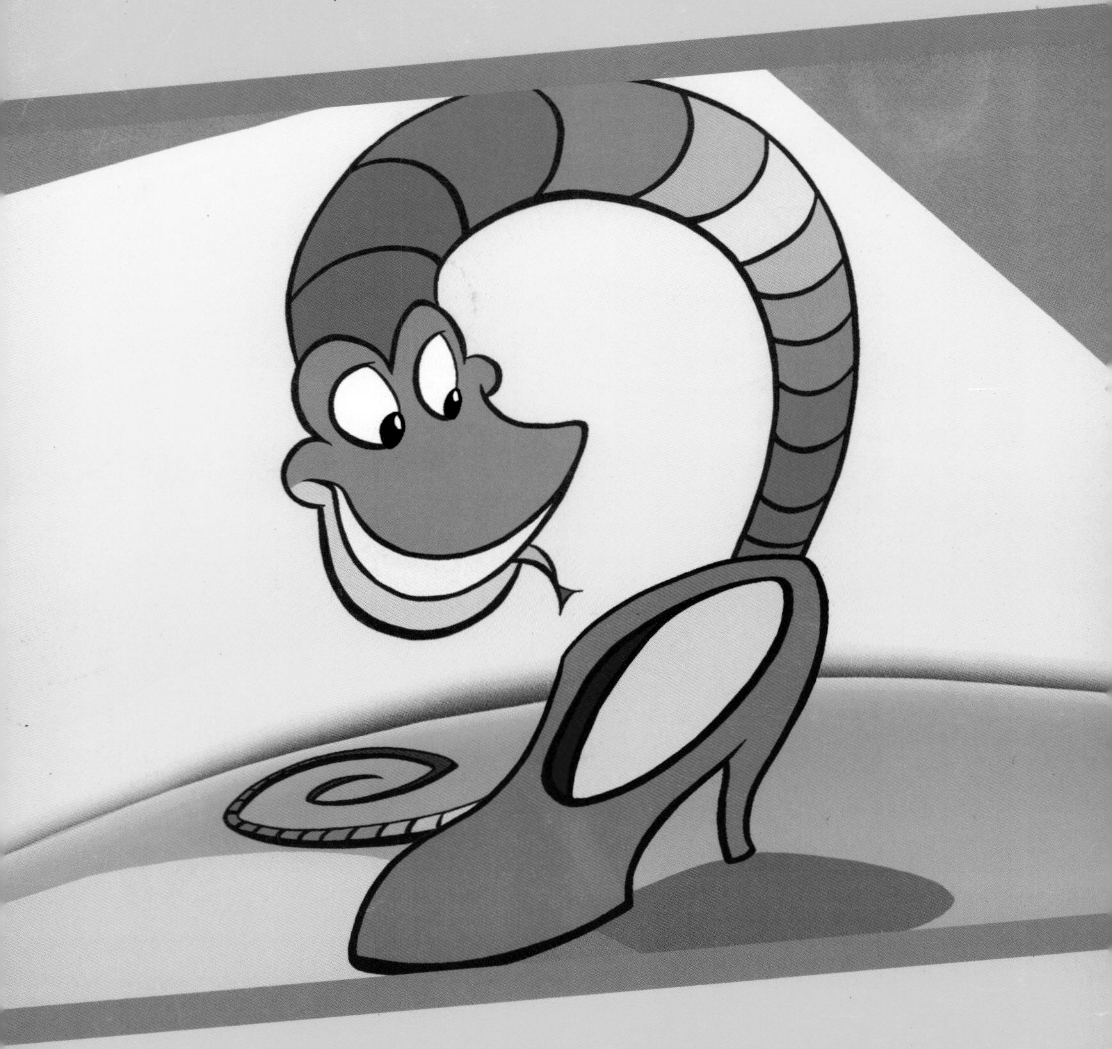

I went in the shoe.

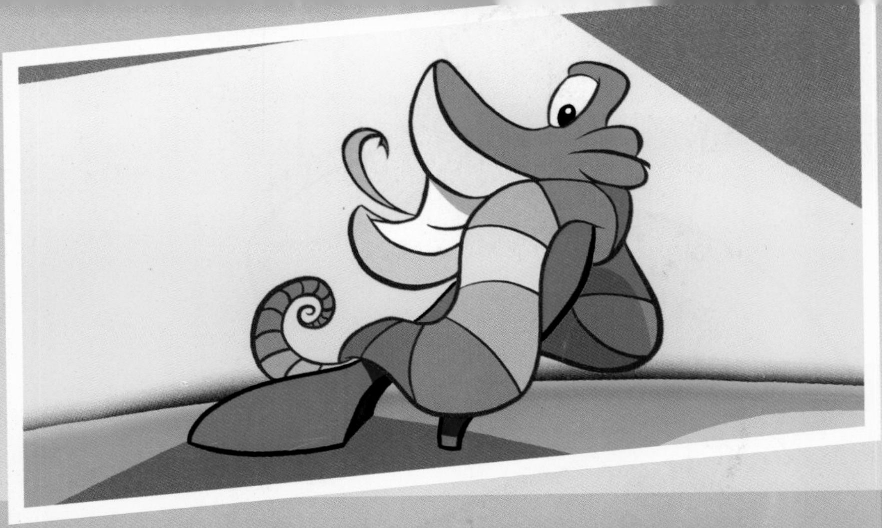

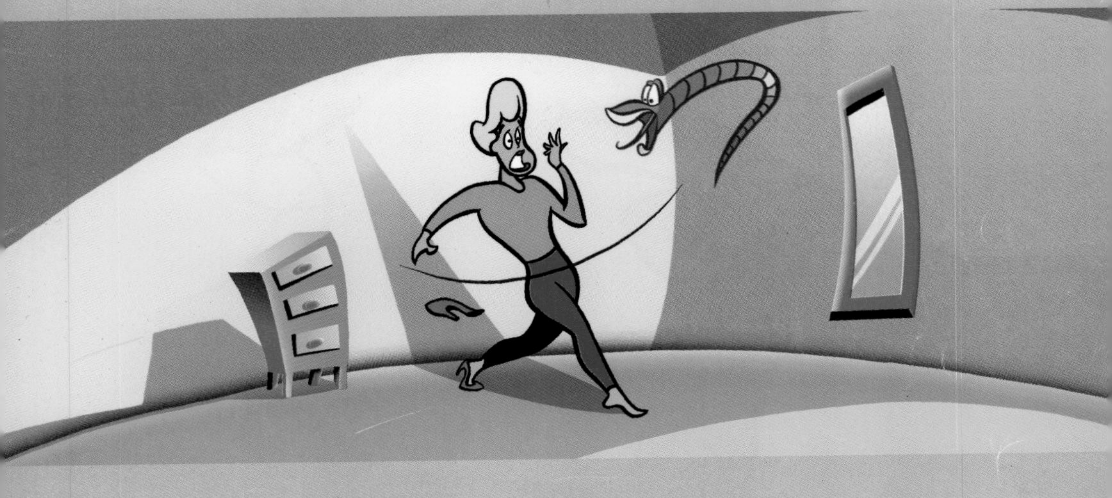

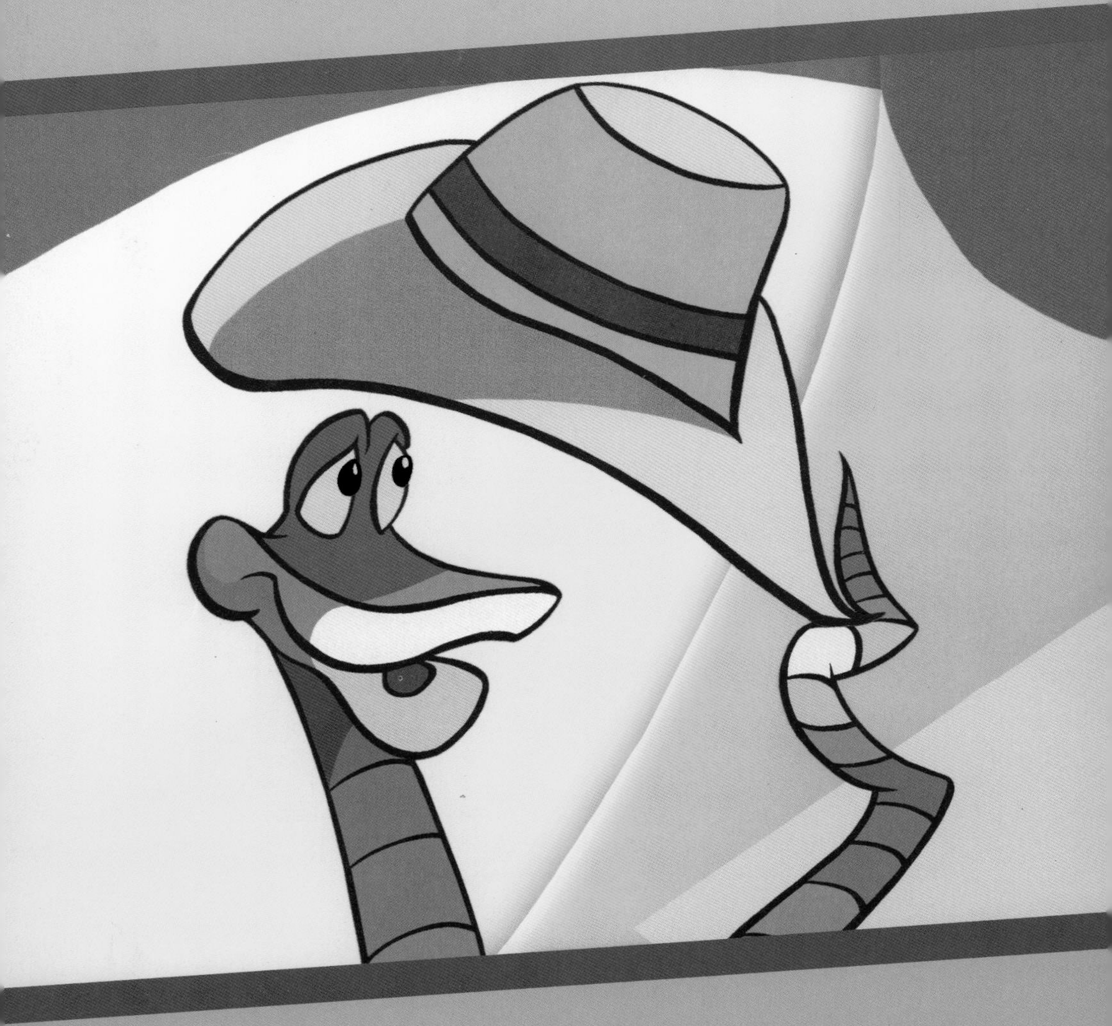

I went in the hat.

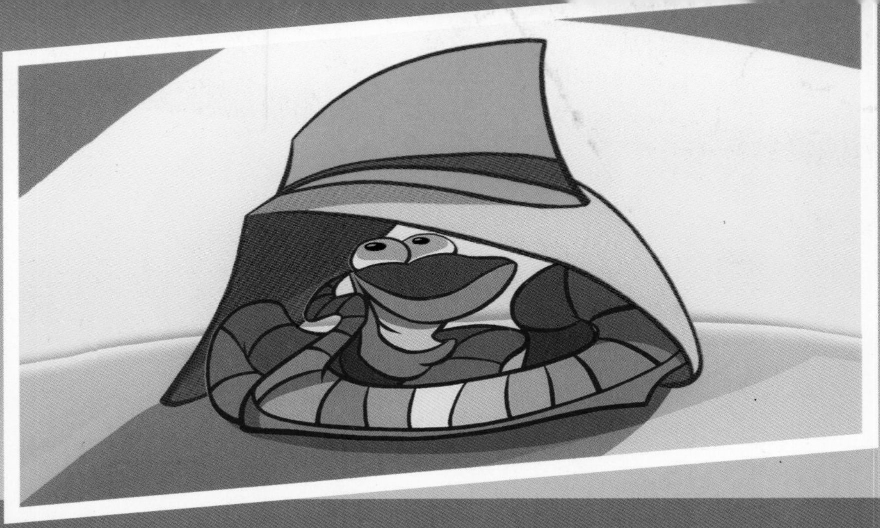

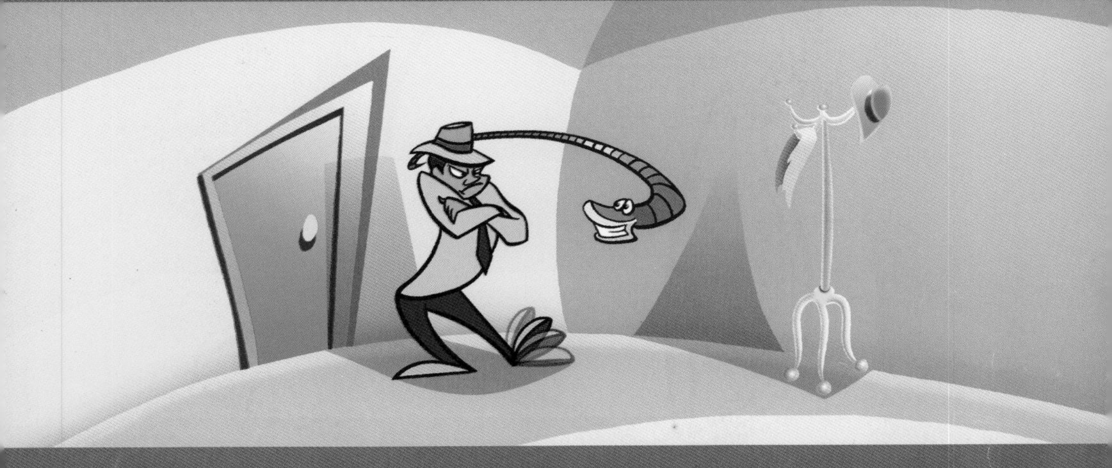

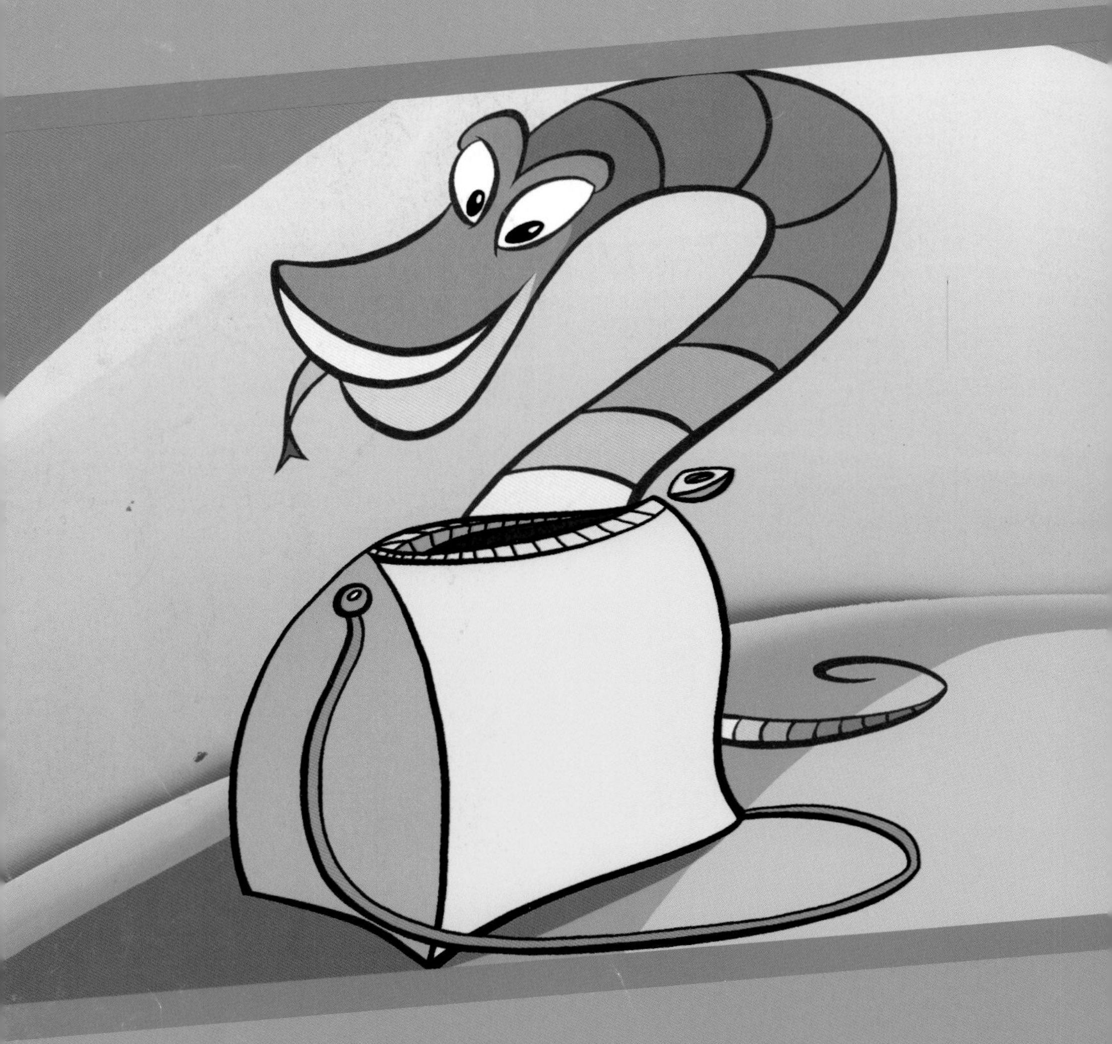

I went in the purse.

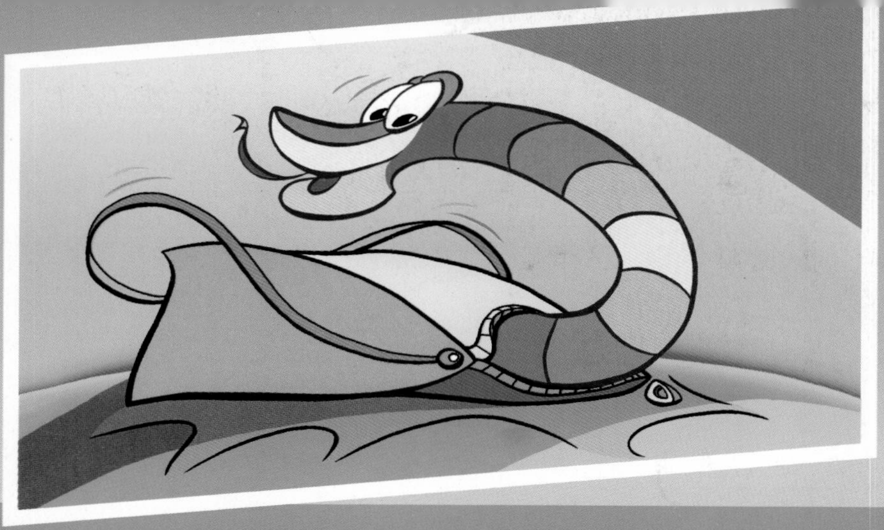

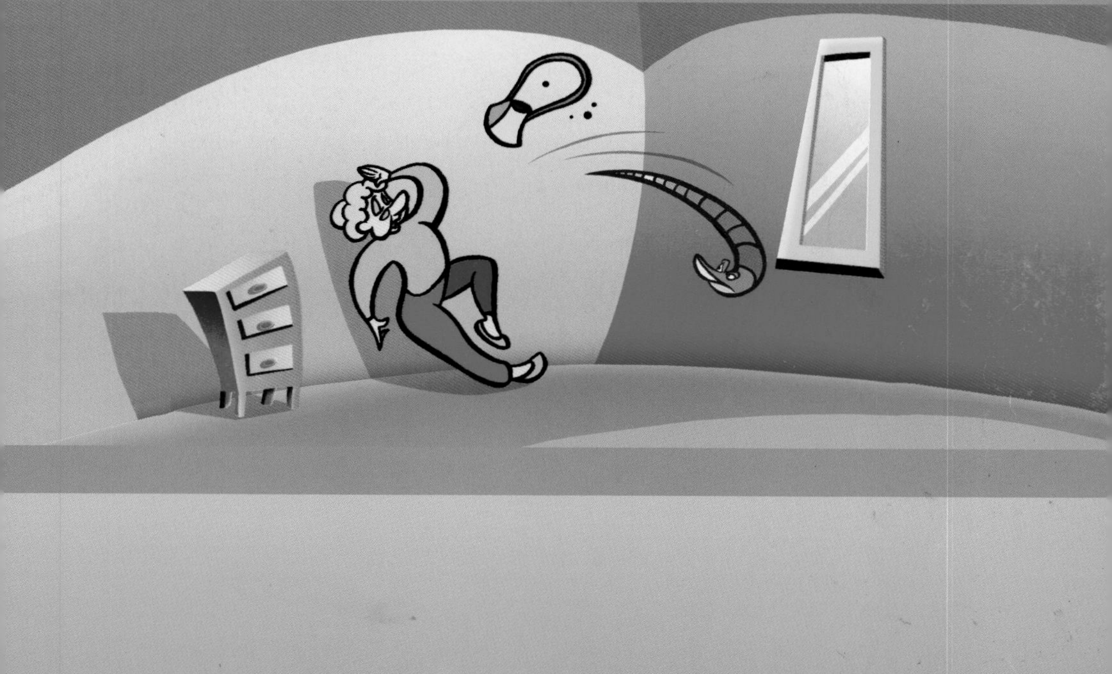

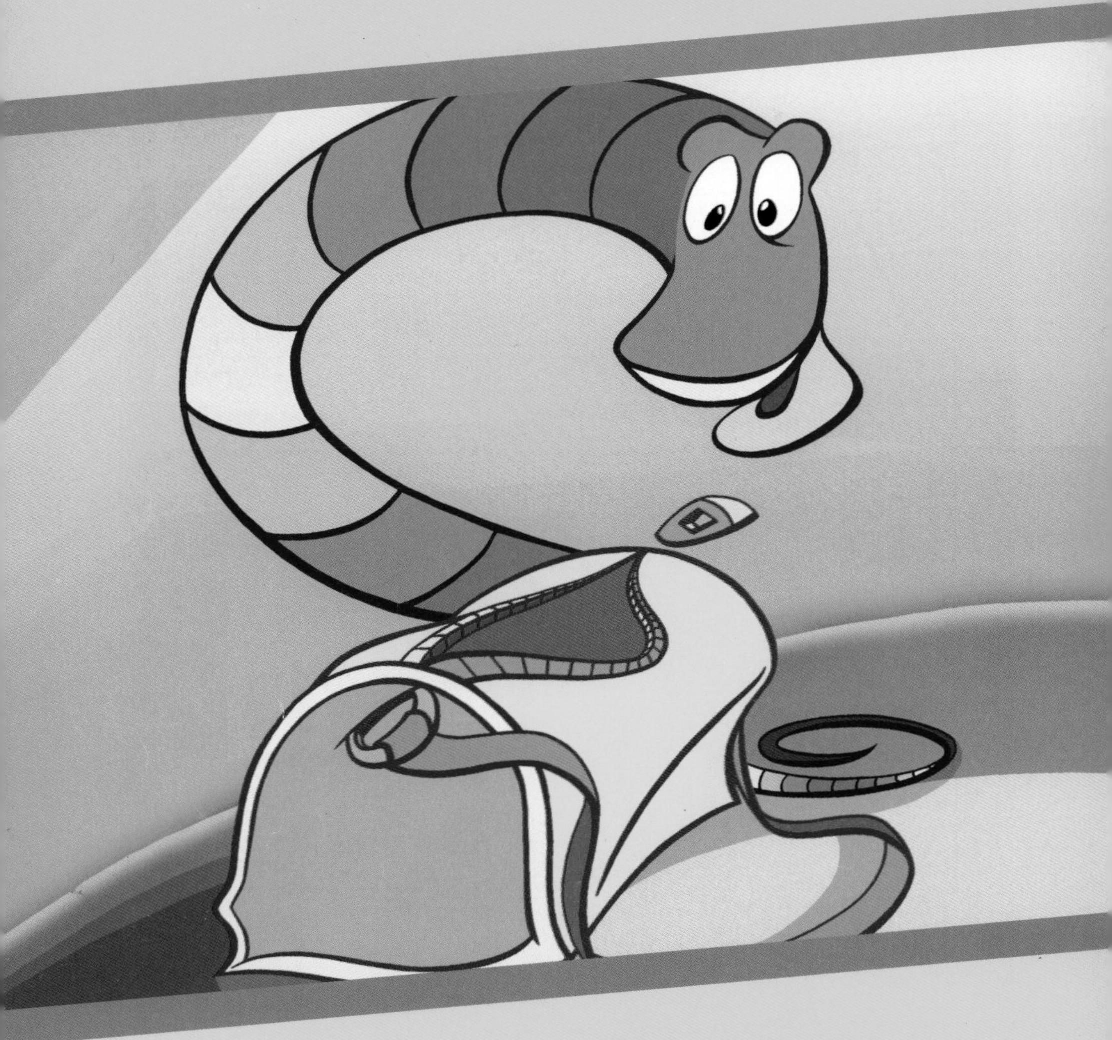

I went in the bag.

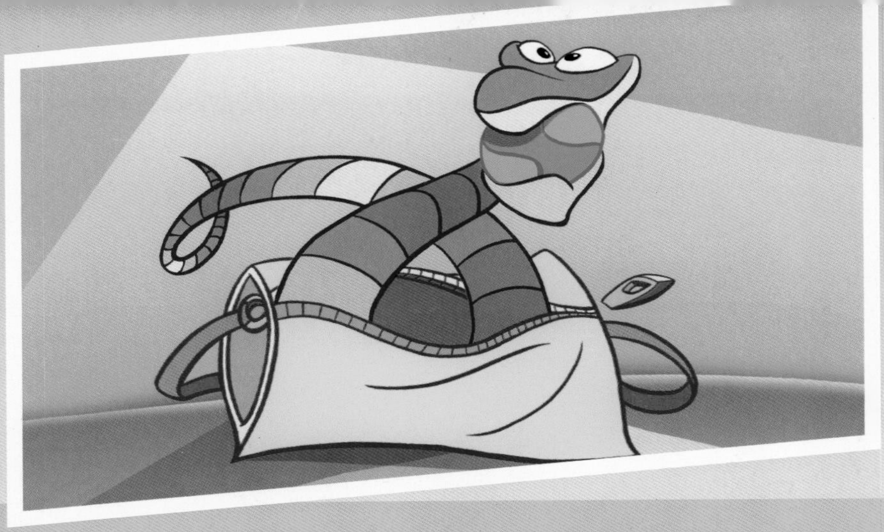

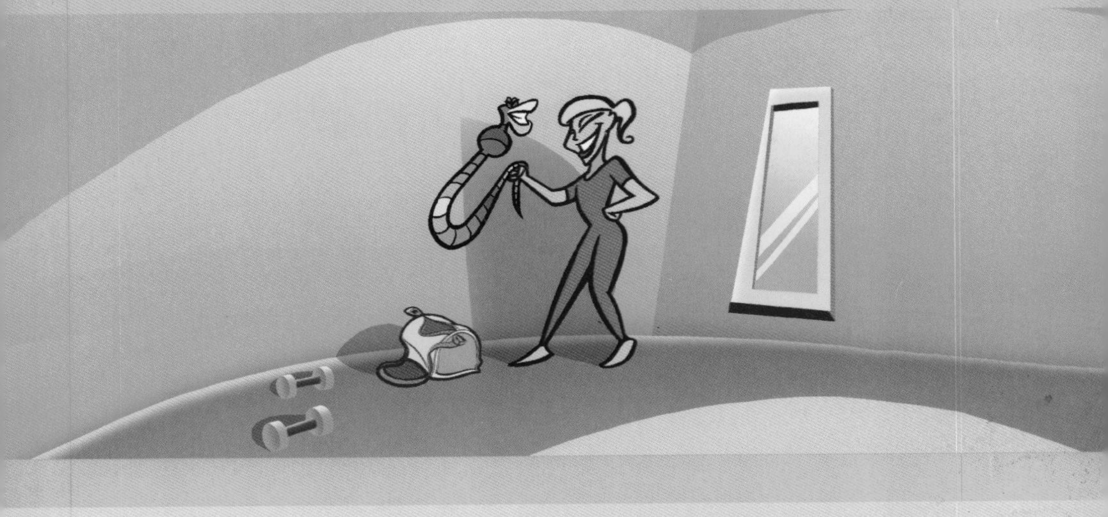

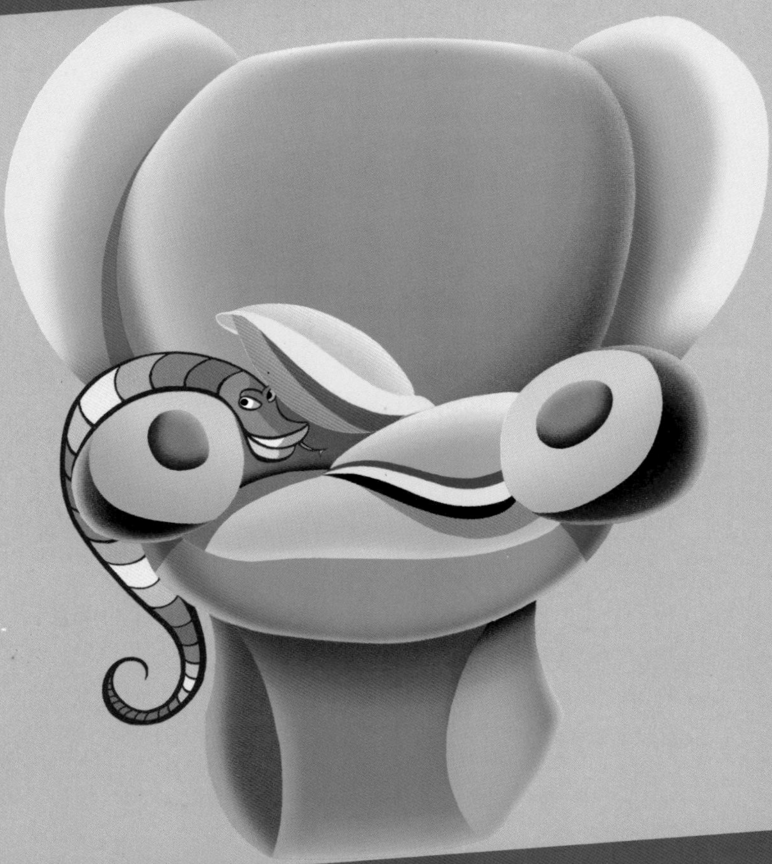

I went in the chair.

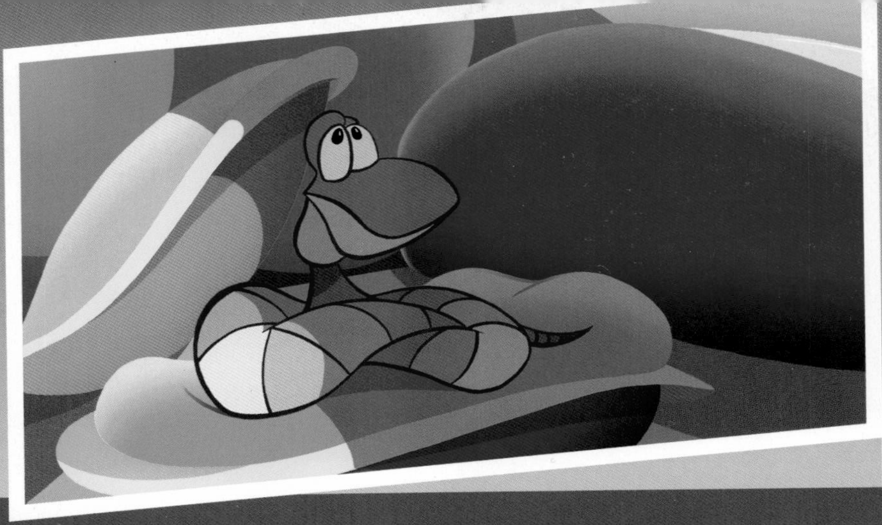

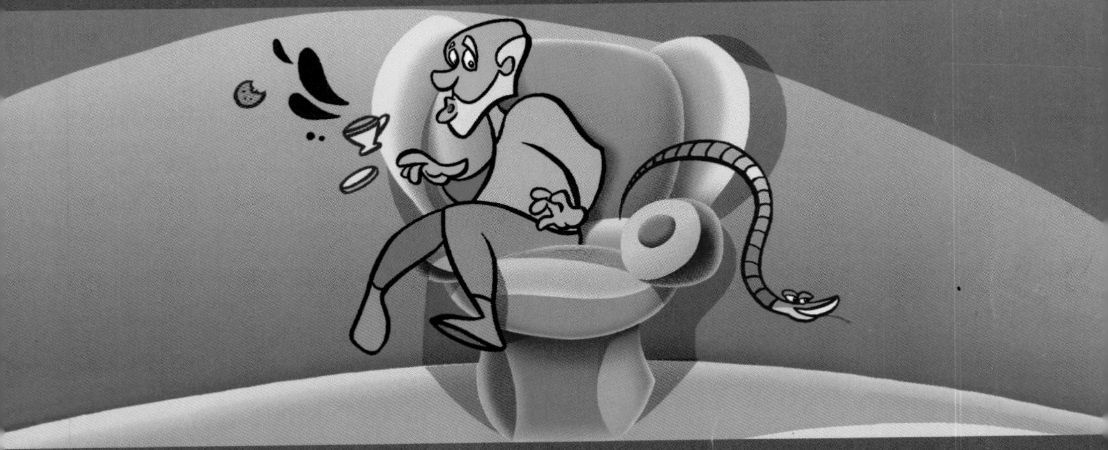

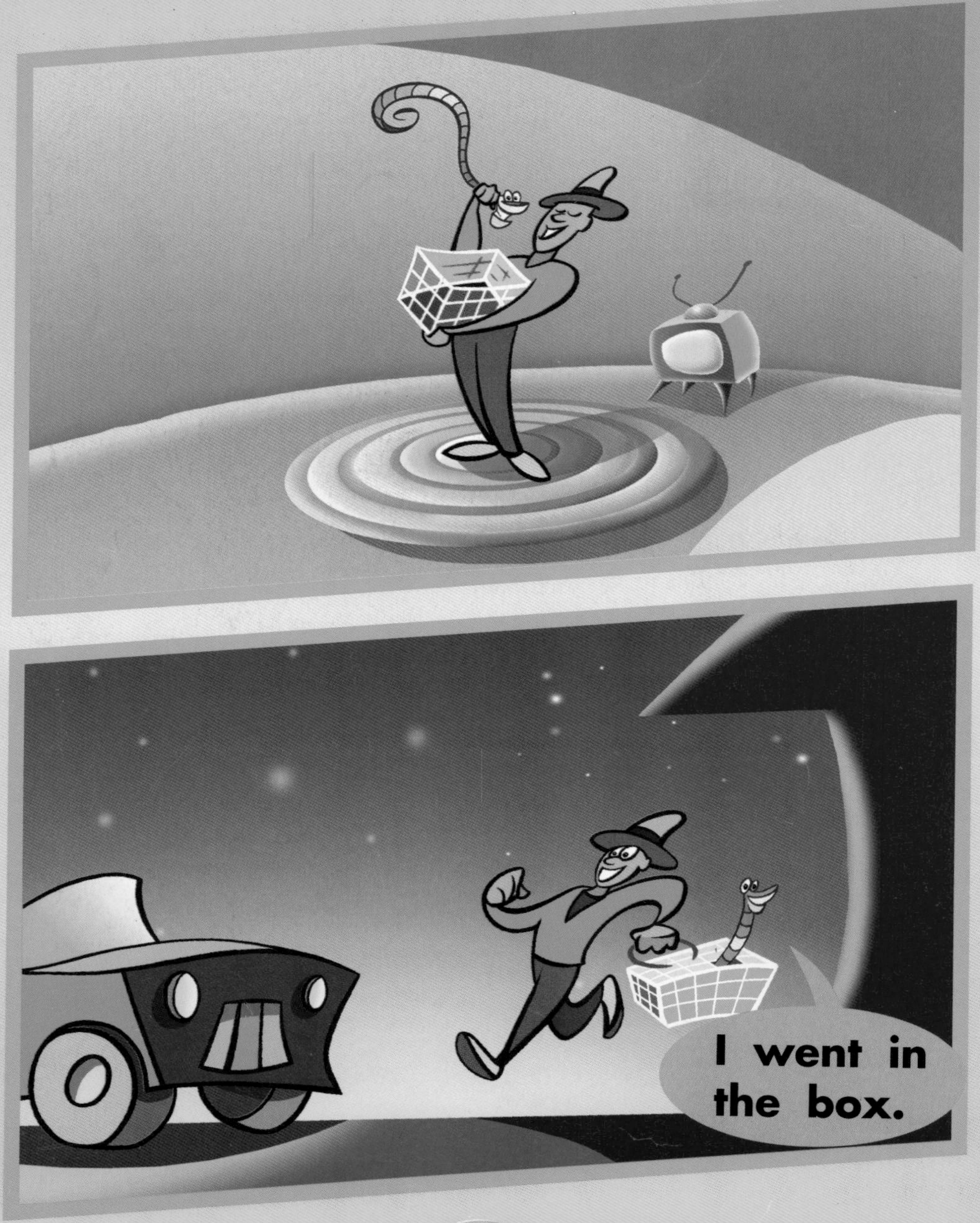
I went in the box.

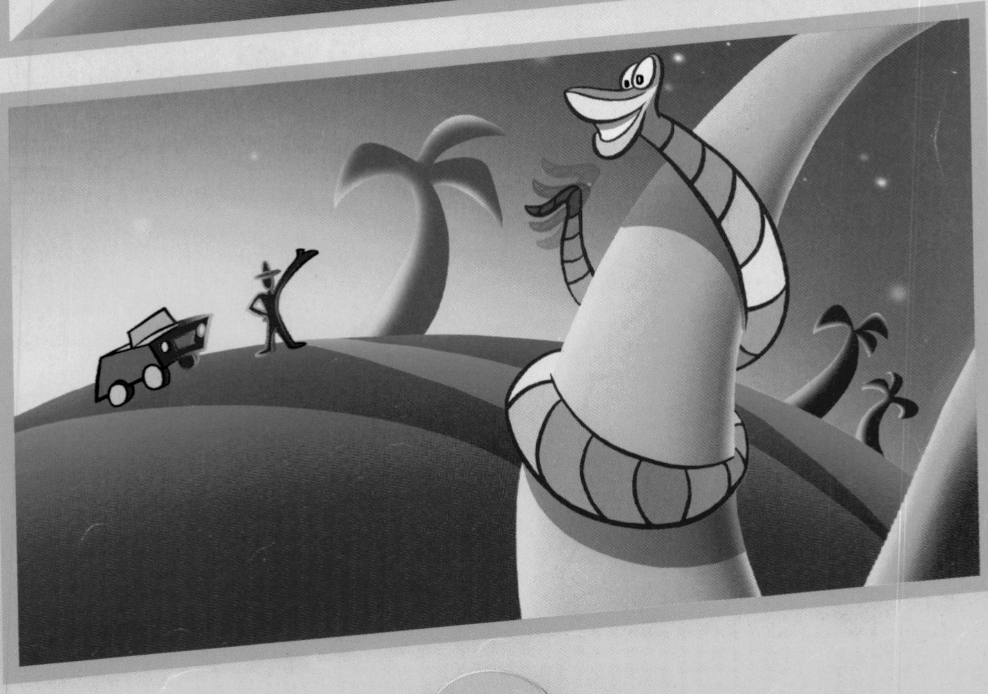

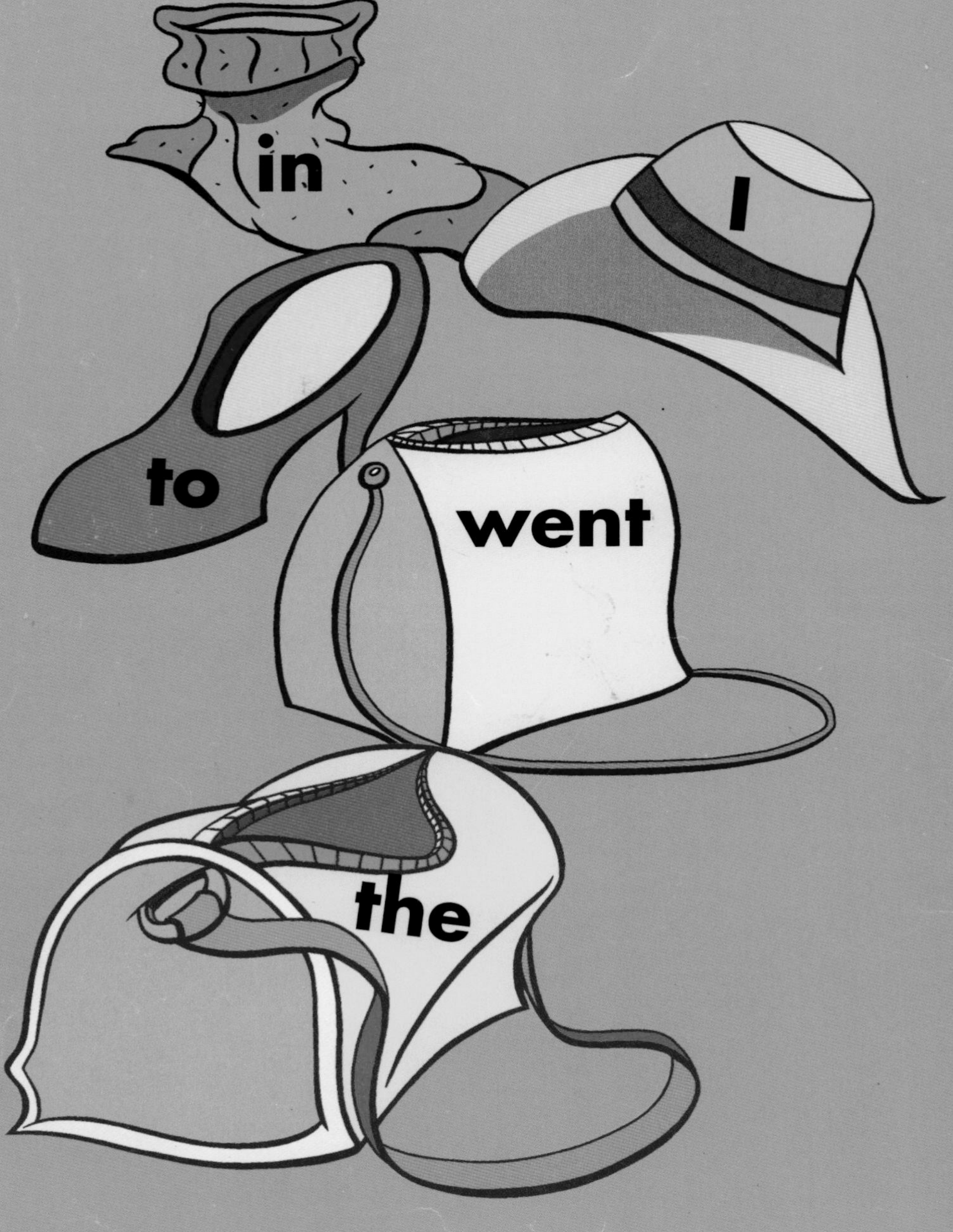
in
I
to
went
the